THE SECRET EXPLORERS
AND THE RAINFOREST RANGERS

CONTENTS

1 Adventure calls   4

2 A meeting with Fig   20

3 The search is on   38

4 A sinister plot   50

5 A snappy escape   64

6 Following Fig's trail   76

7 A desperate plea   90

8 Saving the day   **104**

The rainforests of Borneo   **116**

Animals and plants   **118**

The problem with palm oil   **120**

Quiz   **122**

Glossary   **124**

Acknowledgments   **128**

Chapter One
ADVENTURE CALLS

"There you are!" Ollie whispered with a grin.

The koala he'd spotted didn't seem at all concerned that Ollie was there, sitting below the tall trees. It bit off a fresh mouthful of eucalyptus leaves and munched thoughtfully.

Ollie was at a nature preserve for the day, not far from his home in New South Wales in Australia. Even though there were dozens of koalas living here, you had to be patient if you wanted to see them.

A second gray shape came shuffling down the tree trunk.

Another koala! Ollie thought excitedly. I might even get to see one with a baby!

It was a scorching hot day. Ollie sat cross-legged on the warm ground and took out his carton of apple juice.

The earth was dry and hard, like a cookie that had been baked for too long. But Ollie knew these eucalyptus trees weren't in trouble. Trees were his special interest, as well as the creatures that lived in them. In fact, he knew so much about forests that he sometimes had a very special, secret role to play...

Ollie pictured the trees' roots in his mind. Although he couldn't see them, he knew they ran deep underground. That was how they could stay alive even when the ground was dry. Their long, searching roots could find water deep below the surface and suck it up!

Just like this, Ollie thought, and slurped his apple juice noisily.

The long roots weren't just good for the trees, they were good for the koalas, too. Eucalyptus leaves held lots of water. The koalas could quench most of their thirst just by eating them, so they didn't have to go looking for much else to drink.

Ollie could name all the parts of a tree without having to look them up. The topmost part was the crown. The layer just inside the bark was the cambium, which grew and made the tree get thicker. And the glowing compass on the side of the trunk was...

Wait! Glowing compass?

Ollie leapt to his feet. He had a badge on his shirt that looked just like that. The compass was the symbol of the Secret Explorers! When it appeared like this, it only meant one thing.

A new mission!

None of his everyday friends knew he wasn't just Ollie, the kid from Waratah Street who liked to study trees. He was an adventurer —the Rainforest Explorer.

Ollie ran up to the tree. The glowing outline of a door appeared on it. He pushed it open and ran through into dazzling white light. Strong winds roared around him...

...and the next moment, he was in the Exploration Station!

"Ollie, here!" he shouted.

The Secret Explorers' hidden base had gleaming walls of black stone. On one side were display cases, showing off all the different objects the Explorers had collected. On another side were the computer stations, where every Explorer could help watch over

the missions. The lounge zone had enormous padded armchairs and bulging sofas.

Ollie was the first to arrive. He ran past the map zone, where the floor showed a huge map of the world and the Milky Way glittered from the domed ceiling overhead. He dived into an armchair and watched the other Explorers arrive.

"Connor—here!" The Marine Explorer ran in, excitedly.

A girl wearing glasses jogged in. "Kiki here! Whoa, Connor, careful you don't bump into the machines." Kiki was the Engineering Explorer.

Next to arrive were Roshni the Space Explorer and Gustavo the History Explorer.

"Cheng here!" called the Geology Explorer, who came in and sat next to Ollie.

Next came Tamiko, the Dinosaur Explorer, rushing through the door in such a hurry that she was still chewing a mouthful of dinner. "Tmmkmmf hmmf!" she said and swallowed. "Sorry, guys. I know, I eat like a stegosaurus."

Finally, Leah jumped through the doorway. "Leah here!" she announced happily, and saluted. Leah was the Biology Explorer, an expert in all sorts of plant and animal life.

Leah flung herself onto the sofa next to Kiki. "Any news on the mission yet?"

"Not yet," said Roshni. "I hope it's Mars!"

"Or an underwater volcano," said Cheng.

Connor agreed. "That would be awesome."

They all watched the map on the floor and eagerly waited.

A light suddenly appeared in the middle of an island. It was in Southeast Asia, to the northwest of Australia.

"That's Borneo!" Ollie said at once. He'd know that part of the world anywhere—it was famous for its rainforests.

A shaft of light projected up from the map. At the end was a little square screen like a window. It showed a lush green rainforest.

Sitting among the trees was a young creature with reddish-orange hair. It had long arms, short legs and a mischievous look.

Gustavo was puzzled. "Is that a monkey?"

"It's a kind of ape called an orangutan," Ollie said. "Our mission must be to help it."

But only two Explorers at a time were ever selected. The rest would stay at the Exploration Station. Who would get to go?

Ollie crossed his fingers hard...

The next second, Ollie's compass badge lit up brightly and so did Kiki's. They grinned

at each other
and smacked
their hands
together in
a high-five.

"There's
a big surprise!"
laughed Roshni.
"The Rainforest Explorer was chosen!"

"But why the Engineering Explorer, though?" Gustavo wondered.

"The Exploration Station never gets it wrong," Leah said with a shrug.

Kiki jumped up. "Okay, Ollie, let's get on our way. Time to fire up the Beagle!"

She headed over to a bank of controls and pulled a big lever. A section of the floor opened and a circular platform rose up. Sitting in the middle of it was... a shabby old go-kart.

Of course, all the Secret Explorers knew that the Beagle was a lot more than it seemed...

Ollie and Kiki climbed on board and fastened their seatbelts. The other Explorers took their seats at their computer stations. If there was any trouble during the mission, they would give whatever help they could.

In the middle of the Beagle's peeling dashboard was a big red button marked "START."

Ollie pushed it. The Beagle began to shudder and vibrate. Suddenly they shot

forward into a rippling tunnel of light. The Exploration Station vanished and there was nothing but dazzling brightness and howling wind all around them.

Before their eyes, the Beagle began to change. The cockpit stretched out and became pointed. A clear canopy closed over their heads. Two graceful white wings extended from the sides.

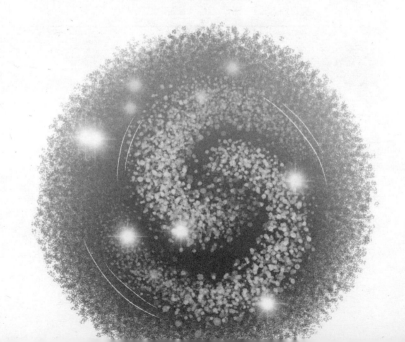

The light faded away. As Ollie blinked the dazzle out of his eyes, he saw clear blue sky outside. Far below were green treetops, pressed thickly together. To his surprise, except for the gentle rushing of wind, everything was completely silent.

"The Beagle's turned into some kind of plane!" he burst out. "But why's it so quiet?"

"Because we're gliding," Kiki explained. "See the controls? This is a motor glider. We only need the engine sometimes."

Ollie took hold of the joystick that had risen up in front of him. He steered the Beagle on a wide circle, taking in the amazing sight of the rainforest.

"Welcome to Borneo," he told Kiki.

"It's beautiful!" she said in awe.

"It is," Ollie agreed. But he knew there must be danger here, too. The Exploration Station had sent them here for a reason.

Somewhere down there, a little orangutan needed their help...

Chapter Two
A MEETING WITH FIG

The Beagle coasted gently through the sky. Ollie and Kiki took in the incredible view.

"Look at all those trees packed so close together," Kiki said, her eyes wide. "I've never seen so much green in my life!"

Clouds floated over the green of the rainforest. "They're made by water evaporating from all those leaves," Ollie said. He pointed out a long, straight gap in the canopy. "That looks like a landing strip."

Kiki nodded. "We'd better touch down so we can get on with our mission. You'll need the engine's power to make a controlled landing." She reached over and switched it on. The propeller shuddered to life.

Kiki showed Ollie where to push the joystick and when to work the pedals. He brought the motor glider around and lined the nose up with the landing strip. The Beagle made a happy little *BEEP* that sounded like "Good job!"

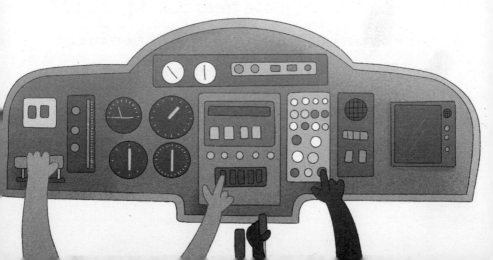

Ollie tilted the plane into a steady descent. Kiki held her breath as the landing pad approached. The wheels bumped the tarmac. Brakes squealed. Steadily, they came to a complete stop.

"Phew!" Ollie gasped.

"Great landing!" Kiki grinned. "Um... any idea where we are?"

Ollie looked out. They had landed alongside a tall security fence. A sign read *"HATALA ANIMAL SANCTUARY AND NATURE PRESERVE"*.

"In exactly the right place, I think!" he said.

Excitement growing, Ollie climbed out of the Beagle, Kiki close behind him. Bird and frog sounds echoed around them, and everything smelled damp and earthy. But most noticeable of all was how hot and humid it was! Ollie felt as if he was walking through steam.

"Whew," said Kiki. "I'm so sticky already!"

They headed over to the double front gate. Through the wire Ollie spotted a boy around his own age, wearing shorts and a cap.

"Come on in," the boy said brightly. "I'm Jamal."

"I'm Kiki, and this is Ollie," said Kiki. "You actually get to work here? I'm jealous!"

Jamal said, "I'm a volunteer. Want me to show you around?"

"Yes!" the two of them yelled together. A private tour of a Borneo nature preserve? Ollie could hardly wait to get inside!

The nature preserve was much bigger than he was expecting. All the animals had plenty of space to move around. Jamal took them to an enclosure with a stream running through it, where elephants were bathing.

The elephants had cute faces with big ears, and long tails that almost reached the ground. "What kind of elephants are they?" Kiki asked.

"Pygmy elephants," explained Jamal. "You only find them here in Borneo."

One of the elephants wandered over to Kiki and sat down in front of her, looking at her with wide, trusting eyes. Kiki flapped her hands in pure delight. "Can I take pictures?"

"Go for it!" Jamal laughed.

Kiki pulled out her camera and took several shots of the little elephant. She'd modified the camera to have a constant internet connection, so all she and Ollie had to do was press a  button to upload them onto his blog. "Your readers are going to love this!" she told him.

"Readers?" asked Jamal.

"My blog. Green Guy Goes Global," Ollie explained.

Jamal led them to the clouded leopard enclosure, where the beautiful wild cats were almost invisible against the undergrowth because of their blotchy fur. After that, they met the silvered langur monkeys. Kiki took dozens of pictures of the gray adults with their orange babies clinging to their tummies.

Ollie felt excited but anxious, too. The nature preserve was thrilling, but he didn't understand what it had to do with the mission.

"These animals are all safe, right?" he asked.

Jamal looked very serious. "They are now."

"What do you mean?"

"All these animals have lost their homes," Jamal explained. "That's what this preserve is for. We take care of them."

Kiki gasped. "That's awful! How did it happen?"

"The rainforest where they used to live has been cut down," Jamal said.

"But why?"

Jamal made a face. "To make room for palm tree plantations. You'd be surprised at how many different things palm oil is used for. Cooking, deodorants, lipstick, fuel... even some chocolate has palm oil in it."

"The plantations create lots of greenhouse gases, too," said Ollie. "And that leads to more climate change. They're a big problem."

As the tour went on, Ollie saw they were coming up to the orangutan enclosure. Kiki gave Ollie a nudge. "This must be where we find out about our mission!"

With Jamal leading, they climbed up a tower to a viewing platform. It offered a superb view of the treetops. Ollie spotted several orangutans up among the branches, swinging from bough to bough with their long arms. He'd never seen these fantastic creatures up close before.

"Do they have names?" Kiki asked.

Jamal pointed to each of them. "Sure! The big old guy is Sibu. That one's Pongo, and that's Betty."

"What about that little scamp?" Kiki took a picture of a young orangutan who was down at ground level. The creature was playing with a collection of odd objects. Ollie saw a comb, several pens, sunglasses, and a flashlight.

"That's Fig!" Jamal laughed. "You have to watch her. She's always stealing bits and pieces from our visitors." He patted his pockets. "Shame I don't have any figs for you to give her. She loves figs. It's why we call her that."

Ollie watched Fig digging into the dirt with the comb. "I think I know what she's up to," he said. "Orangutans are tool users. They use objects to dig up insects and seeds to eat."

"Animals use tools too? That's amazing!" Kiki said. "Whoa! She's coming to say hello!"

Fig had noticed she was being watched. She scrambled up a nearby tree, swung across to the platform, and pulled herself up. Ollie quickly found himself face-to-face with Fig, looking right into her strange, mischievous little eyes.

"She's like a person!" he said.

"That's what 'orangutan' means," Jamal said. "Person of the forest. It comes from Malaysian and Indonesian words."

As Kiki turned to Jamal to ask him more about the palm oil plantations, Ollie suddenly noticed that Fig was reaching out toward Kiki's backpack. Fig rummaged inside and pulled Kiki's camera out. Ollie realized he was watching an expert pickpocket at work!

Ollie gently took the camera from Fig and gave it back to Kiki, who gasped. "Smart girl!" Everyone laughed, and Kiki put the camera back in her pack and zipped up the pocket.

"Come on," Jamal said. "Let's keep moving before Fig steals something else."

Fig climbed down the ladder with them, waving her arms and chattering. Ollie was sorry to leave her behind.

Over the next half hour, Jamal took them to see the pangolins—scaly anteaters that could curl up into balls to protect themselves—and some small black bears with long curved claws. Jamal explained these were sun bears, and were very hard to find in the wild. So much time passed that Jamal suggested they go to the preserve's cafeteria for a break.

While Jamal fetched the cold drinks, Kiki whispered to Ollie. "This is great, but... are you as confused as I am?"

"Yeah," Ollie nodded. "I'm having fun, but the Exploration Station didn't send us here on vacation! What are we meant to do here?"

Kiki shrugged. "All the animals look safe and happy. Could we have come at the wrong time?"

"The Exploration Station doesn't make mistakes," Ollie said.

Just as Jamal sat down with them, one of the adult volunteer workers came running over with a worried look on her face.

"Doctor Faridah," Jamal greeted her. "Is everything okay?"

"Fig's not with you, is she?" Doctor Faridah asked.

"Isn't she in her enclosure?" Jamal said.

Doctor Faridah shook her head. "We've been looking all over for her. And there's a hole under the fence where she likes to play."

Kiki said, "You mean Fig's escaped?"

"That's bad," Jamal said, getting to his feet. A crowd of volunteers quickly gathered, talking anxiously among themselves. The situation sounded very serious. Jamal turned to Ollie and Kiki.

"Fig could be in a lot of trouble," Jamal said. "She's far too young to survive in the wild. I don't know how we're going to do it, but we need to get her back!"

Ollie and Kiki looked at each other.

"I've just figured out why we're here," Ollie said.

"Me too!" said Kiki.

Fig was the little orangutan they'd seen in the Exploration Station. Their mission was to rescue her—and it had just started!

Chapter Three
THE SEARCH IS ON

Now that Ollie and Kiki knew what their mission was, there was no time to lose. They rushed outside, determined to find Fig.

The Beagle was waiting for them on the landing strip. No matter what sort of mission the Secret Explorers were sent on, the Beagle always had the right gear for the job. Ollie and Kiki opened the storage compartments.

They were packed to the brim with rainforest trekking equipment.

"Okay, Rainforest Explorer," Kiki said to Ollie, "what should we bring?"

Ollie carefully picked out what they would need. "Let's start with one good, strong pair of hiking boots each, plus waterproof gear to help keep us dry."

Next came some trekking poles, which are special sticks you could use to keep your balance on uneven ground. Then came hats, sunscreen, sunglasses, and insect repellent. Last of all, they grabbed a map and compass so they could find their way, and plenty of water and food packs to keep their energy up.

"All set?" Kiki asked.

Ollie gave her a thumbs-up. "Let's go find Fig!"

"Hey, Ollie, look at these!" Kiki called. She pointed excitedly at a group of weird-looking purple plants. They were hanging from the trees on tendrils, were shaped like small milk jugs, and had liplike openings at the top.

"Pitcher plants!" Ollie said. "Good thing we're not bug sized, because they'd eat us." He gently showed Kiki the pool of digestive liquid inside one of the plants. "This part is like a stomach. Insects fall in, and the plant eats them."

An unusual-looking tree branch caught Ollie's eye. "Speaking of eating, I think Fig's stopped here for a snack! See how the leaves have been stripped off? Orangutans pull tree branches through their mouths to tear off the leaves."

"We're on the right track!" Kiki cheered. "Hang in there, Fig. We're coming!"

Now Ollie knew what to look for, they could follow Fig's trail. They searched around for more stripped branches and quickly spotted some. They followed branch after branch until they couldn't find any more. Then, suddenly, they smelled a horrible smell.

Kiki held her nose. "It's like poop and onion stew!"

Ollie pointed to a yellow fruit that lay at their feet. Something had pulled off the fruit's spiky rind and eaten half of the flesh. He said, "It's durian. Nothing else on Earth smells like it."

Kiki took a closer look. "I think Fig's been eating it."

It made sense to Ollie that the little orangutan would want to eat fruit as she swung through the rainforest—even fruit that smelled bad to some humans. After all, most of an orangutans' diet was fruit. It was one reason why orangutans were so important to the rainforest. The fruit they ate contained seeds, which passed through

44

the orangutans and came out in their droppings. This meant the seeds were spread around the rainforest.

It was strange to think that one of the things keeping this place so healthy was orangutan poop! But the rainforest would be in big trouble without it.

"Hold still a sec," Kiki told Ollie. "You've got a stick or something caught in your hair."

Ollie waited as Kiki reached out. The next second, she gasped out loud and jerked her hand back. "It moved!"

Ollie froze. Long legs tickled his skin as the "stick" clambered down from his hair and across his cheek.

"That's not a stick," he said through the side of his mouth. "It's a stick insect!"

"Wow!" Kiki said. She leaned in and

carefully lifted the creature from Ollie's face. It was almost a foot long! It crawled onto Kiki's left arm and sat there, gently waving its antennae.

Kiki moved over to a tree and let the giant stick insect climb to the safety of a branch. "We've got to get a picture of this guy for your blog," she said. She reached into her backpack and then cried out, "My camera's gone!"

"Could it have fallen out?" Ollie asked.

"No way," Kiki said firmly. "I zipped this pocket up, but look! Someone has unzipped it."

Ollie pointed out an orangey-red hair caught in the zip. "Hmm. Who do we know who likes to steal things and has hair that color?"

"Fig!" they both said at once.

Kiki shook her head. "Oh, that naughty little orangutan! I bet I'll never see my camera again. She's probably bashing nuts open with it by now."

Ollie sighed. "And it was one of a kind, too. All those cool modifications you made to it."

"Wait a minute," Kiki said. "That gives

me an idea. My camera has a constant internet connection, remember? So if it's still connected, then we might be able to track it!"

"You think if we can find the camera, it might lead us to Fig?" Ollie asked excitedly.

"Yes! But we've got no tracking equipment here," Kiki said. "We'll just have to hope our friends back at the Exploration Station can help..."

Chapter Four
A SINISTER PLOT

"How are we going to find our way back to the Beagle?" Kiki asked. "The rainforest is amazing, but without the GPS on my camera, I don't have a clue where we are!"

Ollie took out the map and compass he'd found in the Beagle's equipment locker. "Ever done orienteering before?"

"Never," Kiki admitted.

"Then this is the perfect time to start!"

Kiki watched Ollie take bearings with the compass and draw pencil lines on the map. "I'd say we're about... here," he said, pointing to where the lines met.

"Wow!" said Kiki. "We've come a long way from the landing strip. I wonder what those buildings are?"

They soon found out. As they hiked through the rainforest, Ollie caught sight of a row of tree trunks, all the same distance apart. That was strange. He beckoned Kiki over to where the oddly neat trees began.

"Oh, no!" he said, as he figured out what they were looking at. "It's a palm oil plantation—like Jamal told us about."

Row upon row of oil palms stood lined up like soldiers ready for inspection. Ollie felt shocked to see how different it was from the rainforest. Only oil palms grew here, without any other plants. There was no diversity, and hardly any sign of animals. The word for that was monoculture.

The rainforest had been a great, glorious mess, like a carnival bursting with life. There was something sad about these quiet, orderly rows of oil palm trees growing where the rainforest had once been. This must be why the animals they'd seen had had to be moved to the nature preserve.

At the edge of the plantation, a row of bright yellow bulldozers had been parked, facing outward. Kiki and Ollie headed over to get a closer look. That was when Ollie heard voices.

"Get to cover, quick!" he hissed to Kiki.

They hid behind the nearest bulldozer, crouching down next to its muddy caterpillar tracks.

Two men and a woman came into view. The woman held a tablet. One of the men carried a clipboard, and the other a phone. He wore dark glasses and seemed to be the leader. He barked questions at the other two as they walked between the oil palms.

"And you're quite certain we will be ready to start by six o'clock tonight?"

"Only one more set of papers to sign," said the clipboard man.

"Get it done. Now, is the expansion zone clearly marked? Signs posted? I don't want the men cutting down the wrong trees. It would be all over the newspapers."

"Taken care of," said the woman with the tablet. "Cheer up, boss. You're looking at a fifty percent increase in palm oil production. You'll be rich!"

"I'm already rich," sneered the plantation boss. "And I'll celebrate when this project is complete, not before!"

Ollie and Kiki traded horrified glances.

"They're going to cut down even more of the rainforest!" Ollie whispered. "And they're starting today!"

"We can't let them do that," Kiki said. "We've got to stop them!"

"Yes! But... how?"

"This is going to take more than just us," Kiki said. "We need all of the Secret Explorers to help with this one."

Ollie nodded in agreement. "Let's get back to the Beagle, and fast!"

Luckily, the plantation boss and his two employees were starting to walk away from them in the other direction. *At least we won't be spotted*, Ollie thought. He took out the compass so he could find the route to the airstrip.

But the heat and the humidity of the rainforest had left his hands sweaty, and the compass slipped from his grasp. He grabbed for it as it fell, but only succeeded in knocking it into the bulldozer's massive front blade. A sudden sharp **CLANGGGG** ran out.

"What was that?" snapped the plantation boss, and froze in his tracks.

The woman with the tablet peered around the side of the bulldozer. She saw Ollie and Kiki crouching there and her eyebrows shot up.

"Someone's spying on us!" she burst out.

The two men charged around to where Ollie and Kiki were hiding. The boss took one look at them and his face screwed up in rage.

"It's just a couple of kids," he growled. "Grab them! They'll wish they'd never set foot here!"

"Run!" Ollie yelled.

He quickly snatched up his compass. Kiki sprinted off into the rainforest and Ollie followed close behind.

Angry shouts rang through the trees. Ollie could hear boots thumping on the rainforest floor as the three adults gave chase.

The greenery got thicker the farther they ran. Soon the ferns and forest shrubs were almost at waist height. The adults pursued them, easily able to keep track of where they'd gone because of the furrow left through the plants.

"Which way?" Kiki panted, as they came up against a thicket of trees.

There was no time to take the map out, but like any good navigator, Ollie had memorized as much of it as he could. He knew there was a river nearby, and if they followed it they would end up back at the Beagle. "Head around to the left!" he told Kiki.

They skirted around the trees and half-ran, half-skidded down a long, muddy slope. Ollie nearly lost his balance, but Kiki caught his arm and steadied him just in time.

Ollie hoped the adults wouldn't follow them onto the dangerous ground. But a quick glance over his shoulder told him they were still coming—and getting closer!

"We've got to shake them off!" he gasped.

The trees they were running through suddenly became a lot thinner. Ollie quickly caught sight of the reason. Just as he'd expected, they'd reached the river. It was broad and muddy brown, churned up in places where it flowed over hidden rocks. Birds with bright plumage flew up, squawking, as he ran toward it.

"Look!" Ollie called out. He pointed to a large mound of mud. A dark hole led into it, with leaves piled all around.

"What's that?" Kiki replied. They were almost at the water's edge. Ollie couldn't see the three adults any more, but the shouts from behind were growing louder.

"It's a saltwater crocodile nest," Ollie said. "There'll be croc eggs in there. That means there are crocs in this river."

"Oh no," Kiki moaned. "First we have to run through this gooey mud, and now there are crocodiles?"

Ollie skidded to a halt. He'd spotted some stones jutting out from the water, forming a difficult but crossable path across the river.

But other shapes were in the water, too. Scaly shapes, with thick tails and long snouts. They were basking in the shallows, lying so still you could have mistaken them for logs until it was too late.

Kiki gulped. "Looks like you were right. There are crocs in the water! Too bad we can't tell them to go after those three behind us."

"Maybe we can," Ollie said. "Let's get across the river, fast. You've given me an idea."

Kiki hesitated. "Are you sure it's a good idea?"

Just then, the three plantation managers burst into view behind them.

"Never mind," she said, "Let's go!"

Kiki took a step out across the water. She reached the first of the stepping stones, steadied herself, and took another long stride onto the next one.

Ollie took a deep breath. With the crocodiles only a few feet away and the furious adults running along the riverside toward him, he took the first giant step...

Chapter Five
A SNAPPY ESCAPE

Ollie and Kiki cautiously made their way over the stepping stones, one by one. Ollie badly wanted to rush across, but he knew it was better to go slowly. A single slip would land him in the water with the crocs.

As he moved from stone to stone, holding his arms out for balance, he glanced nervously down at the crocodiles. They hadn't moved... yet.

Meanwhile, the three plantation managers were catching up. They came scrambling along the river bank, ducking under tree branches and yelling angrily. "There they are! Get them!"

Kiki made a final leap to the other side. She held out her arm and Ollie caught hold of it as he jumped after her. He landed safely, breathing hard. What a relief to have the firm ground under his feet again!

"They're getting away, you idiots!" yelled the plantation manager. "Don't stand with your mouths open like you were catching flies, go after them!"

"Time to give those crocs a wake-up call," Ollie said. "Quick, look for something we can throw in the water."

Kiki looked around and sniffed the air. "I smell durian!" she said. "I'd know that stinky fruit anywhere now. Look, there's the tree!"

They ran over to the durian tree, which was growing near to the river. Ollie and Kiki

quickly pulled down as many of the spiky, smelly fruits as they could. They tore off the skin and lobbed the stinky flesh at the three adults as they came running up to the water.

"Ha! Missed me!" shouted the clipboard man as a glob of durian flesh flew past him.

Ollie whispered to Kiki, "They haven't noticed the crocs!"

"The plan is working," Kiki grinned.

The clipboard man strode on to the first stone, looking confident. Some durian fruit sploshed down beside him.

In the river shallows, the crocodiles began to stir. Yellow, slit-pupilled eyes blinked open. Long tails lashed the water.

The man yelped in alarm and jumped back on to the river bank. A croc lunged up at him and snapped its gigantic jaws in the air where he'd been a second before. The sound was like great shears slamming shut.

"That's quite a bite!" Kiki said.

"The most powerful bite of any animal," Ollie said proudly.

"I told you to go after those kids," the boss shouted to the cowering man. "What's wrong with you?"

The man pushed past him and ran, yelling over his shoulder as he went. "I'm not going back there. Not for any amount of money!"

"Me either!" said the woman with the tablet, and ran after him.

The boss turned back to the river with a curse. And then he noticed the crocodiles... who had also noticed him.

Slowly, the grinning crocs waded up the muddy river bank.

The plantation boss turned on his heel and ran. Ollie and Kiki watched him flee back into the rainforest and vanish from sight.

"Good one, Ollie," Kiki said. "The plan worked perfectly!" She looked down at her sticky, smelly hands. "With just one problem..."

They wiped their hands clean as best they could on some leaves. "Come on," Ollie said. "We need to get back to the Beagle and call the Exploration Station. The Secret Explorers will help us find Fig!"

They set off through the rainforest once more. The river was a handy landmark, and with Ollie using the map and compass to pinpoint their position, they soon found themselves back at the airstrip. There was the Beagle, still shaped like a motor glider. It let out a very relieved **BEEP** as the two Secret Explorers climbed on board.

"Good to see you again too, Beagle!" Kiki said, and patted the console.

Ollie quickly switched on the communications screen. "Ollie and Kiki calling the Exploration Station. We need help."

The other Secret Explorers appeared on the screen. "Go ahead, guys," said Connor. "What's the plan?"

Kiki said, "Fig has my camera, and it's connected to the internet. So it should be possible to track it, right? Like you'd track a lost phone."

"Of course!" Leah yelled. "Genius! Get to your stations, everyone. We're going to find that orangutan!"

The Exploration Station became a bustle of activity as all the kids hurried to their computers. Kiki talked them through what to do. For a few moments, there was only silence, broken by the sound of digital beeps and clicking keys as the desperate search went on. Then...

"Found the camera's signal!" Roshni called.

In the Beagle, Ollie and Kiki cheered. "Awesome!" Ollie said.

But then Roshni frowned. "Wait. No signal. It's gone again."

"Here it is!" yelled Cheng, and everyone crowded around his screen. But the same thing happened again. The signal vanished almost as soon as it appeared.

Kiki leaned into the screen. "Guys, I think I've figured out the problem. Data coverage in this part of Borneo is really weak. The signal isn't strong enough to track."

She sat back in her chair with a heavy sigh. "I was sure that plan would work. I don't know what else we can do. I feel like I've let Fig down!"

Ollie gave her a hug. "We'll just keep trying."

Then Gustavo said, "Hey, look at this. Ollie's blog is updating!"

Everyone looked at the Green Guy Goes Global blog. Sure enough, a new stream of photos had appeared. Ollie and Kiki recognized the pictures Kiki had taken at the nature preserve, but they didn't recognize the odd photos that came after it. They were all shot from funny angles, as if whoever had taken them didn't quite know what they were doing.

Ollie looked closely. There were pictures of a stream, a rock formation that looked a bit like a pygmy elephant, a family of orangutans sitting in the tops of trees, and lastly, a huge smiling face gawking into the camera.

"That's Fig!" Kiki said, and burst out laughing. "And look, she found other orangutans out there. She must have taken these pictures by accident, and the camera just kept on uploading them!"

The Beagle joined in, making giggly little **BEEPS**. Ollie laughed too. He could see right up Fig's nose.

"I've taken some silly selfies before, but Fig definitely wins first prize," he said." Too bad she can't tell us where she is," sighed Kiki.

Ollie looked back at the other pictures. "Or maybe she already has."

Kiki said, "What do you mean?"

"Don't you see? She's left us a trail!" Ollie said excitedly. "All we have to do is find the places that appear in these photos, and they'll lead us straight to Fig!"

Chapter Six
FOLLOWING FIG'S TRAIL

Ollie and Kiki were back in the rainforest, standing in front of the large lumpy rock that looked like a pygmy elephant. Ollie looked down at the tablet in his hand, where he'd saved the photos Fig had taken, and back across to the rock.

"It's definitely the same one," he said. "See how the trunk curves around, and the patch of moss like an eye? I'm sure Fig was here."

Kiki sniffed the air. "Hey, Ollie? Do you smell Fig's favorite stinky snack?"

Sure enough, at the foot of the rock was a half-chewed durian!

"We're definitely on Fig's trail, no doubt about it," Ollie said. "Let's see where she went to next..."

He swiped to the next photo. It was blurry and at a crazy angle, but he could tell it was a gigantic red flower with pale speckles.

"A rafflesia," Ollie said.

Kiki frowned. "How will we find one flower in this huge rainforest?"

Ollie grinned. "It just happens to be the biggest flower in the world," he said. "And it stinks like rotten meat!"

They hurried along, searching and sniffing, until Kiki stopped. She wrinkled her nose. "Urgh! I think I've found it!"

They followed the terrible stink until they reached the plant. They both gasped—the flower was a yard wide!

"Wow," said Kiki. "But why does it smell so bad?"

"It's to attract flies so they pollinate it," Ollie explained. He looked around. Sure enough, the tree branches next to them were stripped bare of leaves.

"Fig's been here," he said. "She ate these leaves, look. Lucky for us she's still hungry."

"But she's not here now! Where can she be?" Kiki groaned.

There was nothing to do but keep looking. They soon found the stream from Fig's photo, but there was no sign of Fig anywhere nearby. The next photo showed something like a fuzzy orange log.

"Is this an orangutan's leg?" Kiki wondered.

"No," Ollie laughed. "It's a pelawan tree. They have bright orange bark. Among all these other trees, a pelawan ought to stand out like a lighthouse."

Ollie was right. They spotted the pelawan easily. But Fig wasn't there. And there was only one photo left. It showed a clearing beside some trees—not much to go on.

Ollie and Kiki looked closely at the photo. "Those are mangrove trees," Ollie said. "They like swampy, salty water."

"I think I can smell a swamp now!" Kiki said, grimacing.

"Me too. Ah, the refreshing aroma of mud and rotting plants," Ollie grinned. "Let's go!"

It was easy to find the mangroves just by following the smell. The ground under them got softer and softer, until the squishy mud went right over the tops of Ollie's boots. The tree roots poked out of the water like snorkels, which Ollie knew was so they could get oxygen from the stinking mud. He stood under the dangling mangrove branches and looked around for Fig.

"I don't see any more clues," he told Kiki. "Can you?"

"Not a thing," she said. "No durian, no stripped branches, not even a footprint!"

"And we've run out of photos." Ollie felt tired and frustrated. He sat down on a fallen log that was half-buried in the swamp, and tried to think where Fig might have gone next.

"She can't just have vanished off the face of the Earth," he said to himself. "Come on, Ollie. Think! If I was Fig, and I was right here in this clearing, what would I do?"

His own words seemed to echo in his mind. Right here in this clearing...

Ollie stood up suddenly. "Kiki, do you think maybe the reason we can't see where Fig went next is because ... she's still here?"

Kiki's mouth made an O. They looked at each other and then slowly peered upward.

Overhead there was nothing but mangrove branches. All the leaves made it impossible to see if Fig was among them. But as they watched, one of the branches shook, as if something was bouncing on it.

"If she's up there, we need to get her down," Kiki said.

"Maybe we can tempt her?" suggested Ollie. "Leave something she likes on this boulder, and hope she comes to check it out?"

"Good idea! But we don't have any figs for her. We don't even have any stinky durian."

Ollie groaned. "I wish I'd thought to pick some up before."

Then Kiki snapped her fingers. "Hang on. Fig loves to steal things, doesn't she? Little odds and ends that she can use as tools?"

"Yes! Like your camera," Ollie said.

"Maybe if we leave a tool out for her, she'll come and take it," suggested Kiki.

They dug through the equipment from the Beagle they'd stored in Kiki's backpack, looking for something Fig might like. Sunscreen was out—she might try to lick it up. The tablet was too fragile. Then Ollie found a bright yellow pencil at the bottom of his bag. "What about this?"

"Let's try it," Kiki said.

Ollie put the pencil down on the log. "I'm just putting this very interesting object down over here," he announced loudly. "Gosh, I hope nobody tries to steal it!"

He went and hid behind a bush with Kiki. Now to see if Fig was interested...

Nothing happened. Ollie wondered if Fig had moved on after all, and they were wasting their time. But just as he was about to give up, there was a rustle from the branches overhead.

A curious little face peeked through the leaves. Kiki squeezed Ollie's arm and they looked at each other excitedly. It was Fig!

But would she be interested in the pencil? Ollie and Kiki watched anxiously, holding their breath.

To their relief, Fig climbed down. She still had Kiki's camera clutched in one hand. With the other hand, she picked up the pencil and turned it this way and that, studying it.

"I think she likes it," Ollie whispered.

Fig jabbed the pencil into the log, again and again.

Kiki stared. "What's she doing?"

"She's digging out insects from under the bark," Ollie explained. "A good sharp pencil is the perfect tool for the job."

Fig looked like she agreed. She picked a fistful of squirming bugs up from the log and ate them.

Ollie and Kiki grinned at each other. At last, they'd found Fig!

Now they just had to get her safely back home...

Chapter Seven
A DESPERATE PLEA

Kiki and Ollie stood under a fig tree, picking as many figs as they could manage. Soon every pocket they had was crammed with sticky, juicy figs. So were Kiki's backpack and the hoods of their waterproof jackets!

Ollie picked one last fig. "I don't think we can carry any more," he said.

"Better get started, then," said Kiki.

They put a fig down
near the mangrove trees,
moved away a few paces
and put another one
down. They kept this up
until they'd made a trail
of figs.

Ollie ran back to the fallen log,
where Fig was still digging out
insects with her new pencil. "This
way, Fig!" he called. "Time for your
favorite food."

Fig didn't look up at first. She still had
plenty of bugs to munch. But then she
stopped and sniffed.

She can smell the fig juice on my hands, Ollie realized. He ran over to the first fig in the trail, and Fig came chasing after him.

She found the fig on the ground, made delighted hooting noises, and stuffed it into her mouth. "It's working!" Ollie cheered.

"Come on!" Kiki called. "Plenty more figs where that one came from!"

Ollie led the way through the rainforest, using his map and compass to keep them on track, while Kiki made sure Fig was still following them. She dropped a fig from time to time. That was enough to keep

Fig following the trail. The little orangutan didn't always eat the figs—some of them got tossed over her shoulder, sniffed, or played with—but she was always interested in them.

"She definitely has the right name, doesn't she?" Ollie said.

"I didn't think anything on earth could love figs this much," said Kiki, dropping two figs at once. Fig finally put down Kiki's camera so she could grab a fig in each hand. Kiki ran back to snatch it up again, with a look of great relief.

When they arrived back at the wildlife preserve, they found Jamal and a crowd of volunteers were still busily checking the buildings and searching the enclosures for the baby orangutan. When they saw Fig was coming, everyone burst into wild applause.

"There she is!" Jamal yelled. "You did it! You really did it!"

Ollie and Kiki were suddenly surrounded by people wanting to shake their hands, pat them on the back, and high-five them. There were smiles all around. Doctor Faridah went over to Fig and whistled. "You've had quite a feast, haven't you? Look how big your tummy is!"

Fig looked up at her and blinked sleepily.

Doctor Faridah gently picked Fig up. "That's enough adventures for one day. Let's check you over."

While Doctor Faridah made sure Fig was totally unhurt, Ollie and Kiki told Jamal all about their trek through the rainforest. When they reached the part about the palm oil plantation, a look of sheer horror came over his face.

"They're planning to destroy even more of the rainforest? And they're starting at six o'clock today? How could they?"

"I know! It should be against the law," Ollie said gloomily.

"It is illegal to cut down trees where orangutans live," said Jamal. "If we had proof that orangutans lived in that part of the forest, we might be able to save it."

"But we do have proof!" Kiki shouted, leaping to her feet.

"You're right!" Ollie exclaimed, when he realized what Kiki was talking about. He looked at his watch and saw it was half past five. "There's still a chance. We've got to get to that plantation, quickly!"

Kiki, Ollie, and Jamal all raced over to the Beagle. The three of them climbed into the cockpit. Ollie started the engine, took the controls, and eased up the throttle. The propeller roared, the plane started forward and picked up speed, the wheels left the ground, and the Beagle bleeped a valiant fanfare—*TARANTARAAAA*!

Ollie flew them around in circles, rising higher and higher. Then, when they had climbed high enough and could see the plantation below, he cut the engine. They glided silently down.

Ollie looked at the beautiful rainforest spread out beneath them, so ancient and yet so fragile. Then and there, he made a promise in his heart: he would save it, for Fig and for all the other animals.

Kiki pointed out a landing strip alongside the plantation buildings. Ollie restarted the engine and brought the

Beagle down to land. He checked the clock.
Ten minutes to save the rainforest.

The wheels screeched on the tarmac.
The second the Beagle stopped, everyone
climbed out and raced over to where
the bulldozers were parked. The adults they
had had a run-in with before were standing
in a group, talking to a woman in a gray suit.

The plantation boss saw them coming and his face twisted in rage. "It's those kids who were snooping around before! Get them off my property!"

"Is there a problem?" said the woman. She had an identity badge on and was holding a stack of papers. Ollie guessed she was some kind of government official. This could be the break they needed!

"No problem at all, Ms. Lau," said the boss. "Boys! The paperwork's done. Fire up the bulldozers!"

"Wait!" Ollie's voice rang out over the roar of the bulldozers. He ran up to the startled official. "You can't let them destroy this rainforest. It's an orangutan habitat, and we can prove it!"

Ms. Lau looked to the boss with a grave

expression. "If what this boy says is true, then the work cannot go ahead."

"There are no orangutans here!" sneered the boss.

"Oh yeah?" Kiki said, stepping forward with her camera ready. She showed the official the photos Fig had accidentally taken of other orangutans while she was running through the rainforest. "See? A whole family is living out there! Proof!"

The boss laughed. "Nice trick, kid, but it won't work. These were obviously taken in the nature preserve."

Kiki triumphantly pointed to the corner of the photo, where her camera displayed the GPS coordinates for each location. "Nope. These coordinates prove they were taken right here! Orangutans live here, Ms. Lau."

The official studied the pictures closely. Ollie, Kiki, and Jamal waited, their hearts racing, while the fate of the rainforest hung in the balance.

Could they really have come this far, only to fail now?

Chapter Eight
SAVING THE DAY

Ms. Lau looked up from Kiki's camera. "The GPS data speaks for itself," she said. "Clearly, this area is an orangutan habitat, and you have no right to tear it down. Switch off those bulldozers immediately!"

"But my plans," spluttered the plantation boss. "My profits..."

"Your expansion plans are canceled as of now," said Ms. Lau. She took the papers from his clipboard and tore them in half.

The boss and his henchmen turned angrily to Ollie, Kiki, and Jamal. "You meddling little brats!" he roared. "Do you have any idea what you've done?"

"Of course they do. They've saved this rainforest!" Jamal grinned. He threw an arm over Ollie and Kiki's shoulders, and they walked back to the Beagle together, feeling like they were walking on air.

Ollie was glad he'd been able to keep his promise. Of course, the bigger fight was a long way from over. Human beings still threatened the rainforest and the animals that lived there, not just in Borneo but all over the world. But this area, at least, was safe for now.

"Mission accomplished!" Kiki said, leaning back in her seat with a happy sigh. The Beagle gave a *DING!* of agreement.

"Great work thinking of those photos with GPS coordinates," Ollie whispered. "The Exploration Station really does pick the right person every time!"

Ollie and Kiki flew Jamal back to the wildlife preserve and said their goodbyes to him and all the other volunteers.

"Thanks for showing us around," Ollie said.

"The animals were amazing!" added Kiki.

"Any time!" Jamal said. "And thanks again, from all of us."

"Especially from Fig!" said Doctor Faridah, holding the little orangutan by the hand. Fig held her other hand out, as if she was waving goodbye.

Ollie and Kiki waved back, and the Beagle started down the runway. As the Beagle roared up into the sky, they kept waving until the wildlife preserve was nothing but a speck in the far distance.

The big button on the dashboard that had read "START" changed to "HOME." Ollie pressed it.

The Beagle shot suddenly forward, accelerating to a blinding speed. The blue

sky changed to a tunnel of brilliant white light, flickering and roaring around them. The Beagle shuddered and shook, changing shape as it flew. The controls disappeared, the glass canopy folded away, and soon the Beagle was nothing more than a scruffy, battered old go-kart once again.

The light faded away. Kiki and Ollie were back in the Exploration Station, as if they had never left. They unfastened their safety belts and climbed out.

All the other Secret Explorers ran down to meet them. "Great mission, guys!" said Gustavo. "I can't believe you saved Fig and the rainforest."

"Yeah, you should get double credit for that one," said Leah.

"And those crocodiles!" said Tamiko with a shudder. "I bet that's what running from velociraptors must feel like."

"So," said Cheng, "what did you bring back for the display cabinets?"

Ollie face-palmed. "Oh, heck! I forgot all about that." He rummaged through his pockets. "I guess we could use... um... this squashed fig?"

Everyone laughed. "I don't think so," said Connor. "It'll get moldy in a few days."

"Don't worry," Kiki said, jumping up. "I've got something much better."

She ran over to the computers, and came running back a few moments later with a printed-out photo. It showed Fig grinning into the camera, with Ollie and Kiki standing behind her, looking anxious, with their hands full of figs.

Everyone passed it around, and burst out laughing as they saw the looks on the faces.

"Fig must have taken this while we were leading her back home," Kiki explained.

"She has a good eye, doesn't she?" Ollie said.

Once everyone had had a look at the photo, he opened up a display cabinet and put it in. It stood on a glass shelf next to a

Roman coin that Gustavo had found, and a foil package of genuine astronaut food collected by Roshni.

It was time to head home again. Ollie walked over to the glowing doorway, paused, and waved goodbye. "Bye, Kiki! Bye, everyone. See you on the next mission!"

"Great working with you," Kiki said with a grin.

Ollie grinned back, smiling. Then he stepped through the doorway and felt the rising wind ruffle his hair. Once again, everything was a whirl of light and sound. And, before he knew it, he was back, standing at the foot of the eucalyptus tree.

He looked up and saw the koalas munching on leaves, living in harmony with their environment, as so many creatures did.

He sat down in a patch of sunshine to watch. In the distance, a kookaburra was calling, and the sound was like faraway laughter. Kangaroos were grazing on the hills in the far horizon. A peaceful, grateful feeling settled over him.

Here in Australia, the ecosystem was every bit as fragile as the rainforest, and needed to be protected just as much—not just for the sake of the plants and animals, but for humanity itself. Mankind would have to change its ways if life was going to continue as it had before. Ollie knew it was up to the young people of the world to do their part.

No matter where you went, under the sea, over the ice, or deep into the forests, the world was full of important, amazing, fascinating plants and animals.

They would always need help to survive—
and the Secret Explorers would always be
there to protect them!

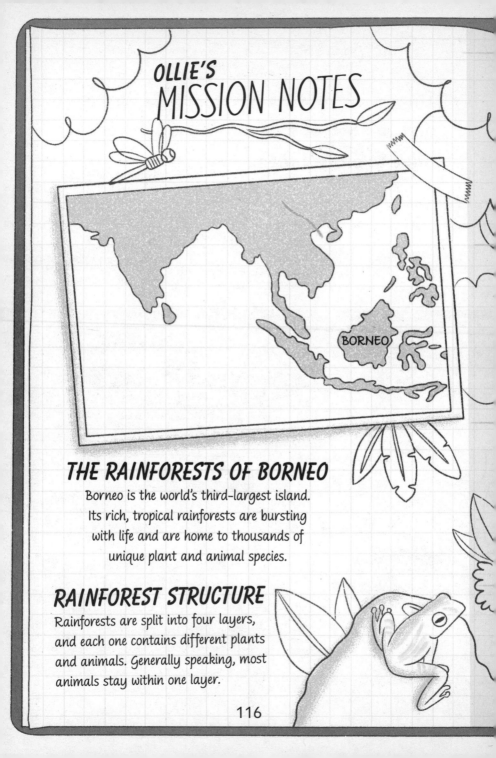

OLLIE'S MISSION NOTES

BORNEO

THE RAINFORESTS OF BORNEO

Borneo is the world's third-largest island.
Its rich, tropical rainforests are bursting
with life and are home to thousands of
unique plant and animal species.

RAINFOREST STRUCTURE

Rainforests are split into four layers,
and each one contains different plants
and animals. Generally speaking, most
animals stay within one layer.

116

EMERGENT LAYER

At the top of a rainforest, the tallest trees poke out into the sunlight. Many tropical birds make their homes here.

CANOPY

From monkeys and bats to lizards and snakes, the canopy is the layer of the rainforest that is filled with most life.

UNDERSTORY

The understory is shady and dry. It's home to many smaller trees and shrubs, as well as frogs, snakes, ants, and termites.

FOREST FLOOR

The forest floor is dark and damp, making it the perfect habitat for insects and insect-eating mammals.

ANIMALS AND PLANTS

ORANGUTAN

* **LENGTH:** Up to 4½ft (1.4m)
* **WEIGHT:** Up to 176lb (80kg)
* **DIET:** Fruit, eggs, insects

FUN FACT: An orangutan's armspan is longer than their height, which helps them reach for branches while climbing.

Orangutans are the largest tree-dwelling animals on Earth, but older males are too heavy to climb very high, so spend most of their time on the forest floor.

PYGMY ELEPHANT

* **LENGTH:** Up to 9¼ft (2.8m)
* **WEIGHT:** Up to 7,000lb (3,200kg)
* **DIET:** Grass, leaves, fruit

FUN FACT: The pygmy elephant is the smallest elephant on Earth. They're only found in the forests of Borneo.

RAFFLESIA

At 3ft (1m) wide, the rafflesia is the largest flower in the world. It's also known as the "corpse lily" because it smells like rotten flesh. It only flowers for a few days a year.

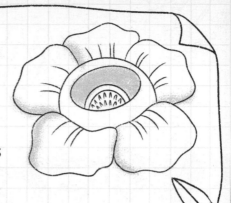

DURIAN FRUIT

Known as "The King of Fruits," durian is so smelly that it's banned on public transportation in parts of Asia. However, despite the smell, many people love its strong flavor.

PITCHER PLANT

The pitcher plant's leaves are shaped like a tube and filled with nectar. Insects drawn to the nectar need to be careful because the rim of the plant is slippery, and if they fall in they will drown in a pool of liquid.

THE PROBLEM WITH PALM OIL

Oil palm trees

Palm oil fruit

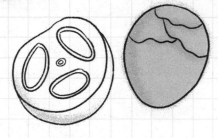

WHAT IS PALM OIL?

Palm oil is a smooth, creamy oil made from the fruit of oil palm trees. It's used to manufacture countless useful products, but there is a huge downside to it.

PLANTATIONS

Oil palms are grown all over the world on huge farms called plantations. To create plantations, rainforests are cut down and replaced with nothing but oil palm trees, destroying the homes of precious animals in the process.

WHY WE NEED TO PROTECT RAINFORESTS

As well as being home to thousands of plants and animals, rainforests also provide many things that help keep our planet healthy. Here are just a few of them:

* **OXYGEN:** Rainforests produce a huge amount of the oxygen we breathe. They're called "the lungs of the Earth."
* **WATER SUPPLY:** Trees help move water from the soil into the air, where it becomes rain and can help prevent droughts.
* **MEDICINE:** Many medicines are made from plants that only grow in rainforests.

WHAT CAN WE DO?

Palm oil is found in a huge number of products, from cooking oil and chocolate, to cleaning products and lipstick. By trying to buy products that are made with palm oil that is grown in a way that is kind to people, animals, and the environment, we can make a difference.

More than 15 billion trees are cut down every year.

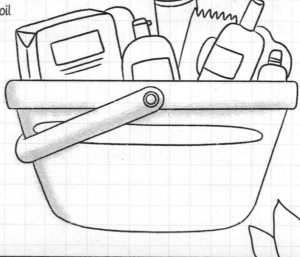

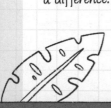

QUIZ

1 How many layers are there in a rainforest?

2 What does the word "orangutan" mean?

3 In which country does Ollie and Kiki's mission take place?

4 Which tree is famous for having bright orange bark?

5 True or false: orangutans can use objects as tools.

6   What is the name of the biggest flower in the world?

7   Which stinky fruit helps the Secret Explorers escape the bad guys?

8   What was the plantation producing?

FIND THE FROGS!

There are five hidden frogs to spot in this book. Can you find them all?

They look like this!

Check your answers on page 127

GLOSSARY

BLOG
An online journal
of information or
images that is
regularly updated

CANOPY
The upper layer
of the rainforest
that contains
the most life

COORDINATES
A group of numbers
used to indicate a
point or position

DIVERSITY
Variety of plants
and animals that
live in an area

DURIAN
A tropical fruit that
is known for having
a very strong smell

GLIDER
A light aircraft that
is capable of flying
without an engine

GPS

A system that helps people determine exact locations on Earth and figure out their directions

GREENHOUSE GAS

A gas in the atmosphere that traps the sun's warmth around the planet, such as carbon dioxide

LANDING STRIP

A runway for a plane to take off and land from

NATURE PRESERVE

A protected piece of land designed to keep the animals and plants that live there safe

ORANGUTAN

A large tree-dwelling ape with long arms and orange fur that are native to Borneo

ORIENTEERING

An activity where people use a map and compass to find their way

PALM OIL
An oil made from the fruit of oil palm trees that has many uses, but is often farmed in ways that are harmful to the environment

PLANTATION
A place where crops are grown

POLLINATE
The transfer of pollen from one plant to another so plants can reproduce

RAINFOREST
A hot, damp forest habitat found in warm climates

TENDRILS
Part of a climbing plant that helps the plant support its weight

Quiz answers

1. Four

2. Person of
   the forest

3. Borneo

4. Pelawan tree

5. True

6. Rafflesia

7. Durian

8. Palm oil

Penguin Random House

For Conall

Text for DK by Working Partners Ltd
9 Kingsway, London WC2B 6XF
With special thanks to Adrian Bott

Design by Collaborate Ltd
Illustrator Ellie O'Shea
Consultant Derek Harvey
Acquisitions Editor James Mitchem
Designer Sonny Flynn
US Senior Editor Shannon Beatty
Senior Production Editor Robert Dunn
Senior Producer Ena Matagic
Publishing Director Sarah Larter

First American Edition, 2021
Published in the United States by DK Publishing
1450 Broadway, Suite 801, New York, New York 10018

Printed and bound in Great Britain by
Clays Ltd, Elcograf S.p.A.

www.dk.com

For the curious

The publisher would like to thank: Sam Priddy and Jo Clark;
Sally Beets for editorial assistance; Caroline Twomey for proofreading.